HOME FARM TWINS
AT STONELEA

Mitch Goes Missing

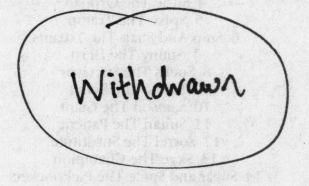

Home Farm Twins

Home Farm Twins at Stonelea

Mitch Goes Missing

Jenny Oldfield

Illustrated by Kate Aldous

*Hodder
Children's
Books*

a division of Hodder Headline

A Catalogue record for this book is available from the British Library

ISBN 0 340 74684 X

Typeset by Avon Dataset Ltd, Bidford-on-Avon, Warks

Printed and bound in Great Britain by
The Guernsey Press Co. Ltd, Channel Isles

Hodder Children's Books
a division of Hodder Headline
338 Euston Road
London NW1 3BH

One

'See you later, Helen! See you later, Hannah!' Mary Moore sang out as she dropped the twins by the gate to Stonelea Cat Sanctuary.

'Bye, Mum!' Helen muttered.

'Bye, Mum!' Hannah mumbled. She scowled at her sister.

'And no more arguing!' Mary warned.

Helen looked aggrieved. '*Us?*' she protested.

'*Argue?*' Hannah echoed, as if she didn't understand the meaning of the word.

'Yes, and I'm serious. You're here to visit Miss Carlton for the day, not to continue World War Three.' Their mother tapped the steering wheel, eager to drive on to Nesfield and open up the Curlew Café for business. 'Listen, girls, if you're not in the mood to help out at the cat sanctuary, just say so.'

'I am in the mood!' Hannah insisted. 'It's Helen who's not!'

'I am!'

'You're not!'

'I am!'

'Helen, Hannah, one more word and I'll make you get right back into this car and drive to the café with me. I'll chain you to the sink for the entire day. At the end of it, you'll never want to see another cake crumb or dirty coffee spoon in your whole lives!'

'Scary!' Hannah had the grace to grin at her mum's dire threat.

Helen backed up against the low wooden gate to the cottage. 'Oh no, not the washing-up!'

'Hmm. At least you agree about something.' Mary glanced at her watch. 'Are you going to come to your senses and forget whatever it is that upset you?'

'It was Helen's turn to muck out Solo's stable,'

Hannah pointed out with another poisonous look.

'Wasn't!'

'Was!'

'Girls!' Mary leaned sideways as if to open the car door and force them to climb back in.

'Sorry, Mum!' they said as one.

'We'll be nice to one another,' Helen promised. She turned and clicked open the latch, and stepped on to the crazy-paved path which led to the little stone house in the hollow.

'I won't say another word. I'll be sweetness and light for ever and ever!' Hannah pressed her palms together and held them up in front of her face. '*Plee-eease*!'

Mary's brown eyes sparkled. 'If not, it's the dreaded kitchen sink!' Then she relented. 'Oh go on. Off you go . . .'

Hannah and Helen shot down the path.

'. . . Have a nice day, and say hello to Lucy for me. Tell her I'll pop in for a cuppa when I call to collect you this evening!'

'Close!' Helen sighed. She'd stopped under the oak tree to catch her breath before they knocked at

Lucy Carlton's door. Above her head, stretched out on a low branch, tail swishing lazily, was a sleepy tortoiseshell cat.

'Mum wasn't serious.' Hannah stooped to stroke a smooth-haired grey cat that had come to twist itself between her legs. The cat purred and rubbed against her. 'It was what grown-ups call an idle threat.'

'The way I heard it, there was nothing idle about it . . . Whoops!' Helen grinned, then neatly side-stepped the start of another argument. 'Hey, that grey cat's new, isn't it? She wasn't here last time we came.'

'So's that black one in the porch, and the ginger one stalking through the long grass over there.' Hannah pointed out more newcomers to the old lady's sanctuary. Then she recognised old-timers such as the lazy old white Persian snoozing on a wooden bench by the stream, and the black-and-white tom sunning himself on a wide stone window ledge.

Cats everywhere; that was what struck the first-time visitor to Stonelea. Cats on the roof, cats in the flowerbeds, cats peering at you from upstairs windows, cats in every nook and cranny of the ancient house.

If someone lost a cat, Stonelea was where they came looking. If they found a stray, here was where they brought it to be looked after by the kind 'Cat Lady'.

Some cats stayed for only a night before their worried owners called to collect them. Others took up residence for weeks on end until Lucy managed to find them a lovely new home.

Occasionally she would even adopt one permanently. 'Who else would want a tatty old thing with only one eye and half a tail?' she would ask. 'He'd be on the scrapheap if I didn't take him in, and we wouldn't want that, now would we?'

The battle-weary cat would be curled on her lap, purring contentedly. *Landed on my feet at last!* he would seem to say. *I get fresh milk at the drop of a hat, a dishful of food whenever I want it. Perfect. Yes, purr-fect!*

'Oh, Hannah, look at the sweet little black-and-white one!' Helen cried now, pointing towards the back door of the cottage. A rambling rose had trailed over the stone porch, its pale pink flowers waving gently in the summery breeze. At the base of the prickly rosebush a tiny kitten had got itself caught up.

'He's stuck!' Hannah realised, darting forward to disentangle the young cat. 'Ouch! These thorns hurt!'

'Don't use your hands, try pushing the branches back with your foot,' Helen suggested. 'That's it. Keep them there. I'll reach in through the gap. Here, kitty, kitty!'

As her sister tweeted and trilled, Hannah gritted her teeth. The rose thorns were tough; they could pierce thick denim and still prick like a hundred needles against her leg. 'Hurry up!' she urged.

Helen went on coaxing. 'Here, little cat! We won't harm you. We just want to get you out!'

The kitten crouched behind the thorny branches, green eyes flashing. He was white and fluffy, with a black patch on one shoulder, dark tips to his ears and one coal-black front paw. 'Miaow!' he cried, cheekily baring his milk teeth and hissing at the giant intruders.

'Hurry . . . up . . . Helen!' Hannah repeated. *Ouch! Ouch! Ouch!*

'I'm doing my best!' Helen was down on all fours, stretching both arms under the rosebush. But the kitten wasn't grateful. He was hissing and spitting and waving his stumpy black tail in real annoyance.

'*Aagh!*' Hannah cried out loud and let the branches go. She rubbed her sore leg hard.

'*Waah!*' Helen yelped, throwing herself headlong on to the grass and rolling out of reach of the spiky tendrils. They had just whizzed within an inch of her face. She jumped up angrily. 'Thanks a lot, Hannah!'

7

'Remember, no arguing!' Hannah cut in.

'Huh!' Dusting herself down, Helen peered under the rosebush. 'I thought you said this kitten was stuck!'

'He is . . . *was!*' Hannah corrected herself. She swallowed hard to see the adventurous black-and-white cat stroll casually from under the rambler.

The kitten miaowed and shook himself – *Fooled you!* – then scampered off across the sloping lawn – *Catch me if you can!.*

Another quick change of subect was required.

'Come on, let's tell Lucy we're here!' Hannah suggested, limping ahead of Helen into the shaded porch. 'The door's open. Shall we go in?'

Helen nodded and pushed Hannah on into the empty kitchen. 'Hello, Lucy!' she called in a loud voice, in case the old lady was upstairs.

Hannah waited by the table, glancing down at a long row of empty food dishes on the floor. One or two hungry cats had crept into the kitchen after the twins and were wandering forlornly from saucer to saucer, sniffing and then padding silently on.

'That's odd.' Helen frowned when there was no answer from the Cat Lady.

'Yeah, Lucy's always at home when we call.' Hannah stepped back out into the porch and scanned the large garden. 'Anyhow, she was expecting us.'

Helen went to the bottom of the stairs and called again. Receiving no reply, she joined Hannah outside. 'Maybe she popped into town for something.'

'And left the door open so anyone could walk in?' Hannah was beginning to suspect that something was amiss.

Helen shrugged. 'You know what Lucy's like. She'd never think that a nasty burglar would break into Stonelea. And if he did, she'd probably invite him to tea and talk him into abandoning his life of crime!'

This picture of tiny, thin Miss Carlton made Hannah smile. She was the lady with a big heart, famous all around the Lakes for her love of animals and cats in particular. 'Now where's that special little ginger person got to this time?' she'd say in her sweet, soft voice, searching under cushions on the cane chair in her cluttered kitchen for a recently rescued cat. 'Oh, there you are, my darling! Come to Lucy and have a lovely, warm cuddle!'

Well into her seventies, Lucy had a soft mass of wavy grey hair. Often dressed in hand-knitted jumpers, velvet trousers and quiet moccasins, she herself reminded Helen and Hannah of a thin but elegant cat.

But where was she now?

'This isn't like her,' Helen muttered, glancing at the washing hanging neatly on the line between two apple trees.

'No, and these cats are hungry.' To Hannah this was the most peculiar thing of all. She watched the lazy tortoiseshell rouse itself from the branch of the oak tree, climb down the trunk, and pad softly towards them. The sleek grey cat, together with the ginger one they'd spotted earlier, had already crowded around their legs, miaowing for food.

'Hann, you don't think . . .?' Helen stopped mid-sentence. For a moment, the thought of burglars, muggers, even murderers fogged her brain. It was the kind of thing you saw on the evening news; a frail old person being attacked and robbed.

Hannah shook her head. 'I know what you're thinking. But listen, before we jump to any conclusions, let's just take a good look round first. You try inside the house. I'll search the garden.'

Helen ran back into the kitchen, kicking the empty saucers in her haste. She called Miss Carlton's name, dashing through each chintzy downstairs room and then up into the flowery bedrooms, where still more cats dozed and groomed.

Nothing. Empty. No sign. From room to room she raced, her mind still crowded with fears, dreading what she might find.

Out in the garden, Hannah went more carefully. 'Lucy!' she called. 'Where are you?'

There was no reply; only the high miaowing of a single cat and the flapping of the large red-and-white tablecloth on the line.

Hannah stepped between the freshly washed items, scanning the long grass beyond the apple trees. White blossom drifted down. She had the smell of washing-powder in her nostrils. Why was that cat crying? Where was the sound coming from exactly?

Frowning, Hannah followed the high, thin yowl across the grass and down the rocky slope towards the stream. 'It's OK, I'm coming,' she told the frightened creature. 'What's wrong? Are you stuck?'

'*Yee-oww!*' Louder now, and coming from the bank of the tumbling stream. '*Yee-owwl! Yee-owwll!*'

As Hannah made it down the hill to the water's edge, a cat shot out from behind a thick rhododendron bush. It was one of Lucy Carlton's adopted warriors; a tough black female with battle scars on her face and a chewed ear.

'Oh!' Hannah stepped back in surprise as the black cat opened her pink mouth and howled. 'So you're not stuck after all!'

'No, but *I* am!' a voice said from behind the rhododendron. It sounded cross and relieved at the same time. 'Well and truly stuck! So stupid of me! Come along, Helen dear, I need some help. This way. Mind you don't get your feet wet . . .'

'It's not Helen, it's Hannah!' Recognising Lucy's

voice, Hannah smiled with relief. Holding her breath, easing round the flowering bush, she followed directions. Then she gasped. 'Miss Carlton!'

The old lady gazed up at her from the ground. She lay on her side, one arm crooked under her head, her feet trailing in the stream.

'Don't look so frightened, dear,' she told Hannah. 'I knew my Sheba would tell you where to find me. All you need to do is run quickly to the telephone and call an ambulance. And don't worry, there's not a shadow of a doubt that I'm going to be perfectly all right!'

Two

'She'll be fine. Miss Carlton is tougher than she looks,' the paramedic told Helen and Hannah.

The ambulance had raced to Stonelea and arrived, siren wailing, only ten minutes after Hannah's frantic phone call.

A man and a woman wearing bright green uniforms had jumped out of the large white van with a stretcher and a medical kit. They'd raced down the garden, scattering cats in every direction, and had quickly assessed Lucy Carlton's condition.

'You have slight hypothermia,' the woman had decided, having discovered that Lucy had lain by

15

the stream, unable to move, since the previous evening. 'It's a good job it was a dry summer's night, otherwise you'd have had real problems coping with the cold.'

'Have I been altogether foolish and broken my hip?' Lucy had asked them, in the same tremulous, slightly annoyed voice she'd used when Hannah had first found her. 'Wouldn't that be silly of me, Sheba? It would teach a stiff old person like me not to go scrambling round the garden at my time of life!'

The battered black cat had miaowed back and gently tried to lick her mistress's face.

The paramedics had told her she must wait and see. 'Let's get you to hospital. They'll have to X-ray your pelvis to find out the extent of the damage. But if I were you, I wouldn't be planning to stray very far from home in the near future.'

'Oh dear, oh dear!' With many sighs and tuts, Lucy had been eased on to the stretcher. She'd lain helpless, her wrinkled face white with pain. Then the paramedics had carried her carefully up the garden.

As the cats had sent up a wail of protest, the old

lady had turned her head in panic to Hannah and Helen.

'Girls!' she'd gasped. 'You must promise me one thing!'

The twins had rushed to her side as the paramedics had slid the stretcher through the back doors of the ambulance.

'It's OK, we'll look after the cats for you!' Helen had promised before Lucy had had time to make her request.

'We'll stay here and feed them!' Hannah felt a lump in her throat as the frail old Cat Lady disappeared inside the van.

'Oh, bless you, my dears. I know my little ones are in safe hands with you!'

The doors had closed and the blue light had begun to flash. And that was when the paramedic had told them that Lucy was a tough old surivor.

'Are you sure you two can cope here?' She checked, before the ambulance sped off into town.

'Yes, we're fine!' Hannah said staunchly.

'No problem!' Helen confirmed.

They squared their shoulders, ready for the task ahead.

But as soon as the ambulance slid away round the first bend, they both sagged.

'Help!' Hannah cried, looking round wildly at what seemed like hundreds of hungry cats. Cats in the cabbage patch. Cats stalking under the tables where Lucy Carlton served afternoon teas. The cheeky black-and-white kitten crouching amongst some bright scarlet poppies, ready to pounce.

'What're we gonna do?' Helen gabbled. She felt as if they needed an army of helpers to keep the cats happy and safe.

'We're gonna feed them!' Hannah decided more firmly. 'If Lucy can do it single-handed, so can we!'

'But how many cats are there? How can we be sure they're all here? What if one runs out on to the road and goes missing? We wouldn't even know!' Helen panicked.

'Hmm.' Hannah saw her point. She took a deep breath. 'I know! Let's—'

'Phone Mum!' Helen cut in, her brown eyes wide and dark.

Hannah nodded and they raced for the phone.

* * *

'Stay calm,' Mary Moore advised. 'You've coped well so far, and it's thanks to you two that Lucy has been taken to hospital where they can look after her and do whatever needs to be done. And you're good with your own animals, so there's no need to panic now.'

'But Mum, there are so many cats!' Helen gasped. A long-haired tabby was winding itself round her legs, miaowing at full volume. A thin, cream Siamese sent up its human-sounding cry.

'Do you know where Lucy keeps their food?' Mary asked.

'Yes,' Hannah chipped in. 'The tins are on the pantry shelves.'

'Then spoon some food into each of the dishes set out on the kitchen floor. The cats will know whose dish is whose. Just don't let the big ones bully the little ones.'

The twins took this in. 'Then we do the same thing with the milk?' Helen checked.

'Exactly. That should keep them quiet for the rest of the day. Meanwhile, I'll get in touch with the hospital for the latest news on Lucy. Oh, and another thought . . .' The twins' mother gave them

the strong feeling that everything was under control. 'I'll call the Eltons and ask them to pop in later this morning. I'm sure they won't mind helping you out.'

'Thanks, Mum!' Breathing a sigh of relief, Hannah set about fetching tins from the pantry and tugging open the ring-pull tops. The sound made every cat come miaowing and scampering for their late breakfasts.

'Yum-yum, Feline Favourites!' Hannah chanted as she set down the first full dishes.

A horde of purring cats descended on the

chunks of food and set about devouring them. Tails up, jaws snapping, they gulped and swallowed.

By this time Helen had joined Hannah. 'Our cat, Socks, loves this food!' she promised the cheeky black-and-white kitten. It had managed to leap up on to the kitchen table and grapple with the fork which Helen was using to scoop the meat from the tin. He batted the prongs with his one black paw, then licked his toes, running up Helen's arm and on to her shoulder as she got ready to lower the dish to the floor.

'Hey, hold your horses!' Helen cried, trying not to tip the kitten from her shoulders. She laughed as he scrambled down and attacked the dish of food, his tail pointed straight up like a radio aerial, his purr churning away like a little car engine.

'Talk about hungry!' Hannah sighed. She filled the last dish and stood back to watch the cats eat.

'This is brilliant, isn't it?' Helen relaxed at last. She counted twenty-three tails pointing towards the oak beams of Lucy's kitchen ceiling, twenty-three heads down and concentrating.

'Yeah!' Hannah agreed. When it came to helping

animals, the girls never argued. 'If only Mum could see us now!'

'Well done!' David Moore looked pleased and proud as he listened to the day's events. 'You're a pair of little Florence Nightingales, rescuing Lucy like that!'

Hannah and Helen sat at the supper table at Home Farm grinning like – well, like Cheshire cats, as their mum pointed out.

'But before you go polishing your halos too hard, you have to take Speckle for a walk up the fell,' Mary reminded them.

'Done that!' Hannah chimed.

'. . . And groom Solo,' David added.

'Done that!' Helen sang.

'. . . And feed the geese.' Their mum ran through the list of evening chores. 'Clean out the rabbit hutch, wash the blanket in Socks's basket.'

'Done that, done that, done that!' they chorused.

'Saint Helen, Saint Hannah!' David mused. 'What did your mother and I do to produce such angels?'

'We just can't help it,' Helen sighed.

'We were born this way.' Hannah's grin had spread from ear to ear.

All day they'd been feeding and tending the cats at Stonelea. They'd rooted them out from under beds to comb through any tangles in their thick coats. They'd checked each one thoroughly for fleas or any other nasty little visitors who might have taken up residence during the hot summer months. And they'd made arrangements with Peter Elton for Lucy's cats to be supervised overnight.

The neighbour from nearby Evergreens had called in to the cottage at lunch-time and promised that either he or his wife Alice would sleep at Stonelea to make sure that none of Lucy's feline friends came to harm.

'But I'm afraid we can only do it for a few nights,' he'd explained. 'Alice and I are closing down the kennels for a couple of weeks and taking a holiday ourselves. We set off for Crete at the end of the week. So Lucy will need to find some other volunteers to help her out when she gets back from hospital.'

This was the one worrying niggle that had stayed in the back of the twins' minds as the day had worn on. And now it resurfaced at the Home Farm supper table as Mary explained the latest news from the hospital.

'The nurse I spoke to this afternoon told me that the X-rays of Lucy's hip look quite hopeful. There's no break in the pelvis, but the left hip joint is dislocated. The doctors have manipulated it back into position, but the orders are that she mustn't take any weight on the joint for at least a week. They'll be sending her home tomorrow with crutches and strict instructions to move around as little as possible.'

Helen and Hannah's faces stopped smiling and grew anxious.

'So who'll look after the sanctuary cats?' Hannah asked. 'It can't be the Eltons. They're busy. And besides, they're going away on Thursday afternoon.'

'If Lucy's on crutches, she won't be able to do all that bending down to feed any cats,' Helen pointed out.

'Aha; "uno problemo"!' David agreed. He ran a hand through his untidy, wavy hair, then thoughtfully scratched the back of his head.

'Yes, I can see we're heading for a heated debate,' Mary warned him with a sideways glance at the now silent twins.

'Poor old lady!' Helen left a significant pause, then sighed dramatically. 'She must be lying awake in her hospital bed worried sick about those cats!'

'Ye-es!' Hannah breathed. 'I bet she can't sleep a wink for thinking about it.'

'Bring out the violins!' their dad muttered, miming a musician scraping a bow across the strings. '*Oh, poor, sweet, leetle old-a lady! Mama mia, what will-a 'appen to zose leetle furry creatures?*'

'Da-ad!' Helen and Hannah complained. 'You could at least get your accent straight!'

'We're serious!' Hannah protested.

'Deadly.' Helen frowned at him, then turned to her mum. 'You know, I've just had an idea!'

'Uh-oh!' Mary braced herself.

Helen ploughed on regardless. 'Hannah and me could—'

'Hannah and *I* could . . .' Mary cut in with a light-hearted correction. 'You could at least get your grammar straight!'

25

'OK, Hannah and *I* could volunteer!' Helen continued, her eyes bright and sparkly.

'What do you mean, "volunteer"?' David asked suspiciously.

'To live with Lucy at her place until she gets better,' Hannah explained. *Great minds think alike!*

'Oh go on, Mum; it's the summer holidays!' Helen coaxed. 'No school. Nothing to stop us staying at Stonelea!'

'Except your own precious animals here at Home Farm,' Mary pointed out. 'Speckle, Socks, Solo . . .'

Hannah's face fell for a moment, then brightened. 'Da-ad!' she began.

David stopped her dead. 'I know; I can easily look after Speckle and Co. I work from home. I can just drop everything and do all your little chores instead!'

'Yep!' Helen nodded earnestly. 'Just think of poor Lucy Carlton struggling about that poky little house on a pair of crutches. And how easily Hannah and *me* could move in and help. We could take sleeping bags. We wouldn't be any trouble to her. And if *we* don't do it, who will?'

'Whoa!' David and Mary begged.

'She'd have to close the sanctuary!' Hannah gasped, her eyes big and soulful. She knew her dad could never resist that look. '*Plee-ease!*'

David hesitated. 'I don't know . . .'

'*Plee-ease!*' Helen echoed.

They crossed their fingers under the kitchen table and prayed hard to be allowed to carry out their mission of mercy.

'Oh, OK!' David weakened and gave in. He made as if to wave a magic wand. 'Cinderellas, you *shall* go to the ball!'

Three

'Think mega big!' Helen told Hannah earnestly. 'Think of finding a new owner for every single stray cat at Stonelea! Think of raising hundreds of pounds for the Cats' Protection League!'

'Hey, steady on!' David warned as he stacked their bags in the boot of the car. 'Don't be too ambitious. And don't storm in there on a mission to achieve everything in five minutes. Remember, Lucy will be getting back from hospital when we arrive, and she'll need to take things easy for a bit.'

'Yes, but that doesn't mean we can't try to find new owners,' Hannah objected. 'I thought

29

that was what a cat sanctuary did!'

She and Helen had talked it over well into the night. They'd stayed awake discussing the detective work necessary to trace back and discover how each resident at Stonelea had ended up abandoned. They would make record cards with names, dates and distinguishing characteristics.

Hannah had described the type of file card they would write out. 'For instance, "Sheba. Arrived such-and-such a date. Brought in by, say, Sally Vincent, the local vet. All black, with chewed right ear."'

'Yeah, and we could take a photograph of every cat for identification purposes,' Helen had added. 'Like a mugshot. And maybe even a paw-print!' She'd drawn on her knowledge of police investigations, gleaned from watching too much television.

She'd fallen asleep eventually, and dreamed of a final scene, after they'd succeeded in tracking down the cruel owner of the mischievous black-and-white kitten. Coming across as a tough but fair female cop, Helen had gathered all the prime suspects in one room and made them sweat.

'. . . And you, Mrs X; you knew full well that the adventurous kitten had escaped into next-door's garden. Yet you did nothing about it. Why was that?'

Beads of sweat stood out on Mrs X's brow. In her dream, Helen had turned into a strange cross between Hercule Poirot and James Bond. Her steely gaze swept round the airless room and lit upon Mr X.

'Mr X, as the original owner of the kitten, it was your responsibility to make your garden kitten-proof! You must take a large share of the blame for leaving a hole in the fence!'

Mr X shuffled and looked down at his feet.

Helen's gaze shifted. 'But it's you, Darren X, who was most to blame!'

Cue dramatic music. The camera closes in on the boy's twitchy features.

'You threw stones at this helpless kitten!' Helen thundered. 'There's no use denying it. We have proof. Be afraid. Be very afraid!'

The excitement of the arrest had woken Helen up and given her more time to plan ways to help the injured Lucy Carlton and her feline charges.

So now she and Hannah were charged up, staring out of the car window with furrowed brows as their dad drove them over Hardstone Pass. High Peak towered on the horizon. Lake Rydal glittered in the valley below.

'We'll have to learn all the cats' names,' Hannah muttered, setting her jaw at a determined angle. 'There are twenty-three; that's almost a whole class at school!'

'We'll have to gather information,' Helen said sharply.

The car cleared the brow of the hill then dipped down towards the town. A winding road snaked ahead.

David drove with brakes squeaking and exhaust pipe rattling until they arrived at the cottage by the stream.

Stonelea sat on the outskirts of Nesfield, set back from the main road in a leafy hollow. Fifty metres beyond, there was a petrol station with large yellow signs, then a small souvenir shop and a terraced row of Lakeland stone houses.

'It looks like Lucy just got back,' the twins' dad

said as he slowed down on the bend, jiggled over the humpback bridge, then pulled into the gravel carpark beside the stream. He pointed out an ambulance making its way past the garage in the direction of town.

Hannah and Helen felt their heartbeats quicken as they stepped out of the car. They could see cats swarming in the garden, even one perched on the wooden sign by the gate which read *Stonelea Tea Rooms*. The marmalade cat watched them arrive, his unblinking green gaze following them as they unloaded their bags and marched down the path to Lucy's door.

'Come in!' called the familiar gentle voice, before Hannah had time to knock. 'Oh girls, how lovely to see you!'

'And you!' Feeling suddenly shy, Helen shuffled into the old lady's kitchen and almost dropped her bag on top of the surprised Siamese cat.

'*Yee-owwl!*' The cat scrambled to the safety of Miss Carlton's lap just in time.

The patient sat in her high-backed cane chair, well-wrapped in a soft blue cardigan. She had a pair of crutches propped against the side of the chair and both feet resting on a low stool in front of her. Her neighbour, Alice Elton, was fussing to make sure she was comfortable.

'Hello, Hannah. Hello, Helen.' The practical kennel owner greeted them more briskly. 'If you'd like to make yourselves useful straight away, there's a pile of washing-up left over from yesterday!'

Helen stared at the groaning sink. 'Washing-up!' she echoed faintly.

The stack of cups, saucers and plates was what Lucy had used to serve afternoon tea to her slow trickle of visitors on the day of the accident.

'Yes, look lively, you two!' David said, his mouth twitching into a smile. 'And be good. Either your mum or I will ring later to check on how things are going.'

'Thanks, Dad!' Hannah muttered.

'Yes; bye, Dad!' Helen gritted her teeth. 'Washing-up!' she repeated in a dismayed whisper. She and Hannah were the caped crusaders, the cat saviours, not skivvies at the kitchen sink.

'Bye, girls!' David said with a cheery wave.

34

Mitch Goes Missing

Hannah stared at the pots and swallowed hard. 'Bags I wash!'

'That's not fair! . . . Oh, OK!' Helen sighed. 'Let's get this over with. Then we can really concentrate on saving a few cats!'

'I've served thirty-eight pots of tea for two!' Hannah told Mary later that afternoon. 'I've buttered hundreds of scones and swatted fifty-two wasps away from the jam on the tables here in the garden!'

'Not quite what you'd expected,' her mum murmured, looking up at the apple blossom and breathing in deeply.

'No. And I've lost count of all the plates I've washed!' Helen added in a deep, glum voice.

'Hmm, washing-up!' Mary's mouth twitched as she stooped to pick up the black-and-white kitten who had spent the day getting under everyone's feet. 'Still, it's all in a good cause.'

'Do you like that one? I found out his name's Mitch,' Hannah told her.

'He's a handful,' her mum said with a smile.

'Yeah, but he's sweet.' Hannah defended the

squirming ball of soft fur, taking Mitch from Mary and giving him a hug. 'Lucy says this one isn't homeless. She's only looking after him while his owner is away on holiday. She comes back late tomorrow.'

'Yes, I couldn't imagine anyone wanting to abandon this little cutie.' Mary gave the kitten one last tickle before she went inside the house to see Lucy.

Noticing Sally Vincent's Land Rover pull up nearby, Hannah and Helen left Mitch to play with the petals drifting across the lawn and ran to meet the vet.

'Open the gate, Hannah!' Sally called. 'I've got my hands full here!'

'What's in the box?' Helen asked.

'What's it look like?' The vet lifted a large cardboard container from her car and carried it carefully down the path.

'A cat?' Hannah suggested.

'Good guess. Hi, Mary. How are you?' Briskly Sally knocked and entered the cottage. 'Hi, Miss Carlton. Can you cope with an extra mouth to feed?'

'Who have you brought me today?' Lucy asked Sally, who put the box by the old lady's feet then opened the pet carrier. Still confined to her chair, Lucy greeted her new charge warmly. 'Oh, it's a little tabby person with stripy legs. Poor little fellow, you've been in the wars!'

The vet lifted the cat from the box and gave him to Lucy. 'He was brought into the surgery yesterday afternoon. Severely malnourished, with a dislocated hip and with some bad bites on his neck and back. The person who found him said there'd been a terrible row inside a lock-up garage and when she went to find out what it was all about, this little chap was lying on the floor in a pool of blood.'

'Yuck!' Hannah grimaced.

'First I clicked the hip joint back into place. Then I cleaned him up, put a couple of stitches into the worst wounds and gave him a tetanus jab. He was on a fluid drip overnight and I reckon he's already well on the road to recovery.'

'Yes, you're a brave little soldier.' Lucy soothed and stroked the new arrival, ignoring Sheba who had come padding in to inspect her latest rival for the old lady's affections. 'Believe me, I know how painful it is to hurt your hip like that.'

'How *is* your leg?' Sally asked in a concerned voice. 'Are you sure you can manage to take in yet another waif and stray?'

'Yes, yes, I'll be fine thank you. Helen and Hannah are my live-in helpers. Today they ran the afternoon teas and they managed perfectly!'

The girls blushed and shuffled.

'Does the tabby have a name?' Helen asked.

Sally shook her head. 'Not so far as we know.'

'Could we call him Corporal?'

'Why Corporal?' Lucy wondered.

'Because he has two stripes on his arm, and you said he was brave,' Helen explained.

'Then Corporal it is!' The Cat Lady smiled and stroked the wounded soldier. 'We're going to feed you, and look after you, and try and find out who did those horrible things to you,' she promised. 'And with a bit of luck, we'll find out who you belong to as well. How does that sound?'

'*Miaow!*' Corporal lifted his chin to gaze at Lucy.

Helen giggled. This was more like it! Here was

a neglected cat who needed their care and affection. It was a case for them to solve. So she glanced happily at Hannah. 'Corporal says that sounds fine!' she said, grinning from ear to ear.

Four

'So Dad called in at Stonelea early this morning to take pictures of Corporal,' Helen explained to her mum.

It was eleven o'clock on Wednesday morning; a busy time at the Curlew Café.

'Yes, very nice, dear.' Mary sashayed round the end of the counter carrying a big tray of coffee and toasted teacakes. She delivered it to a table by the window.

'He used his new digital camera.' Hannah took up the story as she showed her mum the results of their morning's work. The picture of the stripy stray had come out perfectly. The twins had taken the print-out and written a title at the top of the page in big, bold capitals:

INFORMATION NEEDED!

Underneath, they'd printed the words: *Do you know this cat? If so, contact Helen and Hannah Moore at Stonelea Cat Sanctuary: Tel. Nesfield 703654.*

As Mary came back behind the counter in her blue apron, a silver butterfly clip holding her long dark hair neatly in place, she glanced at the small poster. 'Hmm. Sometimes having a dad who's an animal photographer has its uses!'

'Don't you think Corporal looks sad?' Hannah murmured, staring down at the picture. The cat's head was resting on his front paws. His pale yellow eyes stared appealingly at the camera.

Mary was swishing by with another loaded tray. 'Yes, dear, very sad.'

The chatter in the busy café filled the room as Helen and Hannah searched in a drawer by the till for scissors and sellotape.

'I meant to say; was it all right with Lucy for you to come into town?' Their mum bustled back to put money in the till. 'Doesn't she need someone with her full-time while she rests her hip?'

Hannah had laid the poster flat and begun to stick strips of sticky tape to the corners. 'Dad volunteered,' she said casually.

Mary did a double-take. 'Your father . . . *volunteered*?'

'Yep, we roped him into serving morning coffee at the tea rooms,' Helen explained. 'He's there now, wearing a flowery pinny . . .'

'Doing the washing-up!' Hannah giggled.

Mary's eyebrows shot up. 'That must be a first! I can't get him to help me here in the Curlew for love or money.'

Helen shrugged. 'We just told him we had an important case to solve. We said we had to track down Corporal's cruel owners and get the Cats' Protection League to take them to court. And we had to get moving before the trail went cold.'

'So can we stick this poster in your window?' Hannah held it up ready.

'Yes, of course. Make sure it's straight.' Once more Mary had to hurry to attend to her customers. A family group wanted to pay their bill and leave.

So Hannah and Helen looked for a good place in the window, just at eye level. They chose carefully, deciding on the best position to attract the attention of passers-by as they strolled along the lakeside street.

'A bit more to the left!' Helen had gone outside to judge the effect. 'Now up a bit . . . down a bit . . . to the right . . . yep, great!'

Hannah pressed the sticky tape against the windowpane as the departing family filed out. There was a mum and dad and what looked like a grandma, along with four kids. The two smallest were in pushchairs, the next one up was a girl of about four, and the oldest a red-haired boy of five or six.

'Sorry!' Helen sidestepped a pushchair and got out of the way. It was a tight squeeze for the family to pass by on the pavement. One of the little ones was crying, the grandma was fussing over her handbag and umbrella, the red-haired boy tripped over a cracked paving stone and fell back against a lamppost.

'Mind where you're going, Mark!' the dad muttered. 'Now come on, Mum, I've got your umbrella . . . It's not raining . . . No, you don't need it right now . . . Ellie? Where's Ellie? . . . There you are. Hold Mummy's hand . . . Come on, Mark. Look lively!'

Nightmare! Helen grimaced at Hannah through the window. The dad was on the point of losing it completely, while the mum had stepped in more patiently to try and get the grandma moving.

Mark said 'Ow!' and rubbed his elbow. Then he glanced up at the new poster of Corporal taking pride of place in the café window. The boy puzzled over the first word. 'In-for-ma . . .' he said out loud, then broke off.

'Information,' Helen said helpfully. She had an idea that the untidy, clumsy little boy had shown more than passing interest in the picture of the tabby cat.

'Mark!' his dad yelled from twenty metres down the street. 'We're crossing the road to feed the

swans. I want you here right now!'

'Do you know this cat?' Helen said hurriedly.

But Mark quickly (too quickly, Helen thought) shook his head and ran off.

'Why do I think he was lying?' she mused quietly, as Hannah came out to join her. They had more posters to put up in other shops, a lot more work to get through before they returned to Stonelea for lunch.

Hannah paused to admire their first effort. 'What are you on about?' she asked Helen, who was still staring at the large family now attempting to cross the busy road.

'What? Oh nothing. Forget it.' Helen dismissed the vague hunch. 'Come on, let's try the post office across the square. And maybe the Thomases will put a poster in their front window . . .'

Full of bright new ideas, Helen and Hannah waved to their mum and sped off on their quest.

'Mitch, stop messing around!' David Moore pleaded.

The twins had returned to Stonelea at twelve o'clock to find their dad tangled up in apron strings.

He'd finished the morning's chores and was trying to hang up Lucy's pinny, but the kitten had other ideas. The dangling ends had caught Mitch's attention and he'd leaped up at them and was now hanging dangerously in midair.

'Hold it, Dad!' Hannah warned. She darted across the kitchen to rescue Mitch, unhooking his sharp claws and whisking him into her arms.

'That cat must have a death wish!' David

muttered. 'He's already tripped me up while I was carrying two cups of scalding coffee. I even caught him trying to climb inside the washing-machine with a load of dirty tea towels. It was nearly the hot wash cycle for one hare-brained kitten. Lucky for him, I spotted him just before I turned the dial!'

'*Aaw, poor ickle fing!*' Hannah gave Mitch an extra close hug.

' "*Poor ickle fing*" my foot!' David turned to appeal to Lucy, who sat smiling calmly in her cane chair. 'Tell the twins how Mitch has been making me tear my hair out all morning!'

'He is a kitten with a taste for adventure,' the old lady conceded. 'It was chasing Mitch down the garden and trying to persuade him not to go for a night-time swim in the stream that made me take my tumble. Of course, the kitten jumped nimbly from stone to stone, then up on to the bridge, while muggins here was the one who got her feet wet!'

David tut-tutted over Mitch's lack of consideration. But Lucy defended him. 'He only does what comes naturally to a kitten. You'd think that after all these years running the sanctuary I'd have better judgment. I should have known that he was nimble enough to get himself out of a scrape!'

'Anyway, you go home later today,' Hannah reminded Mitch, smiling as his rough pink tongue licked her fingers. 'Do you think you could be on your best behaviour for the rest of the afternoon, so you're still in one piece when your owner comes to collect you?'

In answer, Mitch squirmed free and jumped to the ground. He darted under Lucy's chair and upskittled her crutches. The clatter made a sleeping Corporal jump up from the old lady's lap.

'Nope!' Helen laughed.

'I'm off,' David said rapidly, 'before he breaks anything important; like a valuable vase, or his own neck!'

'Bye, Dad!' Hannah and Helen grinned as they saw him out.

'Say hello to Speckle from us!' Helen cried after him.

'And Socks, and Solo, and . . .'

'Yeah, yeah!' He waved back and climbed into the car.

As he drove off, the girls sighed and turned back in to the kitchen.

'Bags I hang out the tea towels.' Helen was the first to pull her thoughts round from their lovely speckled Border collie up at Home Farm. She dragged her feet towards the washing-machine as the telephone started to ring.

'Well, I'd better answer that,' Hannah sighed. After one night away, she too was missing their animals.

'Hey, maybe someone's seen our poster!' Helen came back to life. She hustled Hannah in a race for the phone.

Hannah got there first. 'Hello, Stonelea Cat Sanctuary.'

'This is Joanna Day. I'm Mitch's owner.'

'Ah.' Hannah shrugged at Helen and mouthed the words, 'Mitch's owner.'

'How's my little terror been behaving while I've been away?' Joanna inquired.

'Fine!' Hannah's voice came out high and strained.

Right at that moment, Mitch was involved in a wrestling match with a wet tea towel that Helen was removing from the washing-machine.

'You're sure he's not been any trouble?' his owner persisted.

The kitten rolled himself up in a tea towel, then wriggled free. He crept under it, so that all Hannah could see was a squirming hump under the checked cloth. Then both cat and cloth began to move rapidly across the stone-flagged floor.

'No trouble!' Hannah assured her, trying not to laugh.

'. . . Because he can be a little nuisance sometimes,' Joanna Day went on. 'But in any case, Lucy will probably be relieved to know that I'm coming to collect him at six o'clock this evening, on my way home from work.'

'Thanks, I'll tell her.' Putting down the phone, Hannah watched a grumpy, sleep-tousled Corporal begin to stalk the mobile tea towel. Then she saw Lucy's other favourite, old Sheba, join in from the opposite direction. Together the two big cats crouched, ready to pounce.

'Uh-oh!' Helen held her breath. From under the cover of the towel, Mitch couldn't see the approach of the enemy. He continued to flip around underneath his new plaything, making funny shapes as he rolled and twisted.

Slam! Sheba and Corporal jumped and landed with all their weight. They trapped Mitch under the tea towel and listened to him squeal.

'*Mee-ooww!*'

'One squashed kitten!' Helen cried.

Hannah dived to rescue him and the grumpy Corporal and Sheba reluctantly gave way. They growled, then padded off towards Lucy.

'Come here!' she scolded, accepting first Sheba then Corporal on to her small lap. 'You're big bullies, both of you!'

Hannah scooped up a dazed Mitch from the floor, laughing at him as he shook his white whiskers and flicked his black-tipped ears. 'We'll miss you when you go home!' she cooed.

Helen picked up the trampled tea towel and let it dangle beten her thumb and forefinger. It was covered in paw-prints; a sorry, mangled sight.

Mitch Goes Missing

'Yeah, we're really gonna miss you, Mitch!'
she echoed. 'Like we'd miss a hole in the head!'

Five

'It's amazing!' Helen remarked as she sat cross-legged on the grass and carefully combed through Corporal's thick fur.

'What's amazing, dear?' Lucy sat in the sunny doorway, gently stroking Sheba and looking out at the other cats snoozing, stalking or playing on the lawn.

'How quickly Corporal has got better since Sally Vincent found him.'

The battle-scarred tabby's eyes were brighter, the cuts on his neck already beginning to heal.

'Yes. All he needs now is fattening up, plus a good helping of TLC.' The Cat Lady stroked the black cat with a soft touch. 'Tender loving care is what we all need, isn't it Sheba?'

'You know what, Hann?' Helen looked up at her sister, who was trying to tempt Mitch out from his hiding place in Lucy's rose garden.

'Here, kitty, kitty!' Hannah was on all fours, holding out a tasty morsel in the palm of her hand. Mitch the Mutineer peeked out from under a giant leaf. His ears twitched, his green eyes gleamed.

'Hannah, I've just had an idea!' Helen finished with Corporal and let him escape from her lap to stroll across the lawn.

'Not now!' Hannah countered. 'I'm busy. Here, Mitch! Here, kitty!'

The black-and-white kitten squatted down, eyes on the tasty titbit. Hannah held her hand steady. Mitch edged forward from under the thorny rosebushes.

'Good boy! I only want to tidy you up a bit before your owner comes to collect you!' Hannah coaxed.

Mitch shimmied forward into full view, crouched down, with his rear-end waggling.

'Watch it. He looks like he's stalking your hand!' Helen warned.

Too late. *Pounce!* Mitch made his move.

'Ouch!' Hannah snatched her hand away and let the cat biscuit drop to the grass. Mitch snatched it and scooted out of sight under a flowering currant bush.

'Hmm.' Lucy observed the kitten's antics with a wry smile. 'I think it was the word "tidy" that did it!'

Hannah stood up straight. 'Shall I leave him for a bit?'

'Yes, we've plenty of time to get Mitch in order. Let Helen explain her idea. She's bursting to share it with us.'

Helen nodded and set off at a gallop. 'It's this. Y'know our "Information Needed" posters? Y'know that little kid who looked at the picture outside the Curlew? And y'know I said I thought he recognised Corporal?–'

'Slow down!' Lucy interrupted and Hannah took the time to explain about the large, unruly family who had made their exit from their mum's café.

'A little red-haired boy?' Lucy echoed. 'With

three younger brothers and sisters? No, I'm afraid that description doesn't ring a bell with me.'

'Maybe they're day-trippers,' Hannah suggested.

'Well, anyway . . .' Helen was eager to carry on. 'You remember the rowdy stuff on the pavement? All about umbrellas and the little one in the pushchair crying. So we didn't really get the chance to ask the boy if he recognised Corporal . . .'

'Mark,' Hannah interrupted. 'His name was Mark. At least, that's the name his dad yelled when he wanted him to catch up.'

'Right; Mark. Well, the more I think about the look on his face when he was trying to read our poster, the more convinced I am that he *did* know who Corporal was.'

'But he denied it,' Hannah pointed out. She had half an eye on Mitch, who seemed to have grown bored with skulking under the flowering bush and was currently prowling after a large bumblebee which had just alighted on one of Lucy's sweet-scented honeysuckles.

'Yeah, but there was just something about the way he ran off.' Helen held stubbornly to her theory. 'So anyway, my idea is to ask Mum to look in her till to see if the family paid their bill by cash or credit card.'

Her mind still wandering with Mitch and the giant bee, Hannah shrugged. 'What on earth for?'

'If it's by credit card, we get to know the family's name and other details, like where they live, if we ask Mum to phone the bank!'

Hannah frowned. 'Sounds against the law to me.'

But Lucy was more interested in Helen's idea. 'It's possible that this little boy has some useful information,' she agreed. 'And perhaps he was too young to read the words, so he was confused, and, as you say, in a hurry.'

'Or maybe he was feeling bad about the way they'd treated Corporal; locking him up in a garage and leaving him to starve to death!' Helen's mind took off on another tack. 'If you'd been cruel to an animal, you wouldn't want to own up about it, would you?'

'That's true,' Lucy said thoughtfully. 'But we mustn't jump to too many conclusions. It's possible that poor Corporal was locked in by accident and his owners have been worried sick about him for days and days.'

'Then why hasn't someone come to Stonelea asking about him?' Helen wondered. 'Everybody in Nesfield knows that this is the place to come looking for your cat if it goes missing.'

By now, Hannah too was drawn into the debate. 'Listen. We don't know for sure that Corporal was actually locked inside the garage,' she pointed out. 'All we know is that he had a fight with another cat in there and that someone heard them, found him injured and took him to Sally.'

'Yeah, but that doesn't alter anything. So we can still ask Mum about how Mark's dad paid the bill. That's a start, isn't it?'

Lucy and Hannah agreed.

'Why not phone now?' the Cat Lady suggested.

So Helen and Hannah hurried to pursue their inquiries, while Lucy sat on with Sheba in the sunshine.

When the girls came back out five minutes later, the old lady was taking a cat-nap herself. She woke up with a little start. 'Well?' she asked, trying to read the expressions on their excited faces.

'The family's name is Leyburn!' Helen reported.

'He paid by plastic and Mum remembered how much they'd spent, so it was easy to track down what they were called. She says she doesn't know the name and she didn't recognise the mum and dad or the kids, but she thinks she might have served the old lady before!'

'So the grandma probably lives in Nesfield, and the rest are most likely visiting her for a holiday.' Hannah went on to explain the next part of their theory. 'Say it's Mark's lot who own Corporal, and they brought him along to visit. But Corporal doesn't know the town, so he goes out one day and gets lost. But no one in the neighbourhood recognises the cat, so they ignore him. And the Leyburns haven't heard about Stonelea, so they don't come looking for their lost cat.'

'What about Grandma?' Lucy cut in. 'If she's local, wouldn't she have told them about the cat sanctuary?'

'Well, Grandma's a bit . . .' Hannah hesitated, looking for a nice way to put it.

'Doolally?' Lucy helped her out.

Hannah blushed and nodded.

'Which would mean this has all been an

accident, and the Leyburns didn't mistreat Corporal after all, and they're worried sick about him going missing, and Mark was too young to understand our poster, and all we have to do now is find out whereabouts they're staying, then we can wave our magic wand and take Corporal right back to his worried owners!' Helen paused for breath at last and let Hannah take over.

'So what we do now is look in the phone book for a Mrs Leyburn; Mark's grandma. We find out her address and go and pay them a visit . . .'

'Unless her name isn't Leyburn, which it wouldn't be if she was Mark's mum's mum, because then it would be something different, and we'd be a bit stuck because we wouldn't know what other name to look for!' Helen jumped in again.

'. . . But we're going to try Leyburn in the book anyway, because it was Mark's dad who called the old lady "Mum", so we're hoping she's *his* mum, and not Mark's mum's mum . . .'

'Oh dear!' Lucy cried. 'I'm lost!'

It all made perfect sense to Helen and Hannah.

'We'll explain later!' Helen cried. She was about

to dart back into the house when she caught sight of Mitch balancing on the handrail of the small wooden footbridge which crossed the stream at the bottom of Lucy's garden. 'Uh-oh, Mitch is up to his tricks again,' she pointed out.

Hannah spotted him doing his tightrope-walking act over the fast-running water. 'Shall we run and fetch him?' she asked Lucy.

The old lady nodded. 'He's much too adventurous for his own good.'

So the girls forgot about the detective stuff for a moment and hared down the lawn to rescue Mitch.

They ran by the noisy Siamese strolling haughtily through the long grass, and past the marmalade cat who sat licking his paws under the shade of an oak tree. Other cats wandered by with half a glance at the antics of the acrobatic kitten on the bridge.

'Mitch, come back here!' Hannah scolded as she reached the bank of the stream. She began to pick her way along the mossy stones towards the footbridge.

'Don't move in too fast or you'll scare him,' Helen advised.

But Mitch the Fearless kept his balance on the narrow handrail and walked on over to the far side.

'Come back!' Hannah squeaked.

The far side of the stream was blocked off by a gate and a barbed-wire fence, and was out of bounds for Lucy's cats. Beyond the fence was a wilderness of nettles and brambles, mixed in with some unsightly rubbish tipped by the managers of the petrol station next door.

Mitch flicked his tail, turned to the twins with a disdainful glance, then jumped down from the rail and vanished into a bed of nettles.

'Oh no!' Helen was more annoyed than worried. This meant they would have to run up to the main road and cut back down the side of the garage forecourt to try and head off the kitten. She led Hannah up the bank, along the path and out of the garden, sprinting as fast as she could.

'Hey!' The man behind the till in the garage shop spotted them and assumed they were up to no good.

'Sorry! We've lost a cat!' Hannah gasped. She wasn't looking forward to swiping aside nettles and crawling over a load of rubbish to fetch Mitch back.

'Those cats are a blinking nuisance!' the man called after them. He was small and overweight, with a grey moustache and large-framed glasses. 'I can't stand 'em myself; nasty smelly things digging up my flowerbeds!'

Hannah and Helen ignored him and ran on. Hesitating for a second to identify the area they needed to search, they then took the plunge through waist-high brambles.

'Here, kitty, kitty! Here, Mitch!' Hannah stooped to peer through the undergrowth.

There was a rustle of green leaves, then a blackbird broke cover and flew off over the stream.

'Hmm.' Helen frowned. 'Bird in the bush equals no kitten in the vicinity,' she said in her sharp-as-a-razor detective voice. 'Meaning, Mitch has gone further than we thought.'

Hannah said they would just have to widen the search.

'Here, Mitch! Here, kitty! . . .'

No good. Five, and then ten minutes went by without a sign of the missing kitten.

'What are we gonna do?' Helen sighed. She was hot and sweaty, and her arms were scratched to pieces by the brambles.

Hannah snatched a dock leaf growing nearby, then straightened up to rub it on a pink-and-white raised rash on her elbow. Some stinging nettles had whisked against her during the search. 'What time is it?' she groaned.

'Two o'clock . . . Here, Mitch!' Helen went on grubbing around in the overgrown patch of wasteland.

'That's only four hours until Joanna Day gets

here to collect him!' Hannah pointed out, feeling a knot of anxiety tighten in her stomach. She pushed on through the bushes.

Helen took a deep breath. 'Don't worry, we'll find him!' But where? Glancing up at the tall trees, then peering afresh through the sprawling wilderness, she managed to sound more confident than she felt.

'We *have* to find him!' Hannah insisted. Since Lucy's accident, Mitch had been their responsibility. His owner would never forgive them if she arrived at Stonelea to find that her precious kitten had gone missing.

Helen glanced at Hannah, who stared back with a worried frown.

'Here, kitty! Here, Mitch!' they cried together. They dropped to their hands and knees, hoping for just one glimpse of black-and-white fur, a paw-print, a flash of green eyes, to tell them where the missing kitten had got to.

Six

'A white kitten with black ears?' The man who worked in the garage paid attention to Hannah and Helen's description of Mitch. A white plastic badge on the man's lapel told them that his name was George.

They'd given up searching amongst the nettles and dashed into the shop to ask for help. 'Yes. And with one black front paw!' Hannah added. She was out of breath and her stomach was still knotted up with worry.

'Well, why didn't you say so earlier?' George snuffled his nose and waggled his moustache like a small terrier. The eyes behind the big glasses were grey and blurred. 'I could've told you you were wasting your time down by the stream.'

Helen stared at him. 'You mean, you saw Mitch?'

'I certainly did. He shot out from under those nettles and straight across my forecourt. Nearly caused an accident with one of my regular customers. Mrs Avery had to brake hard to miss him as he streaked out on to the road.'

'Oh!' Hannah gasped as the picture of Mitch swerving clear of car tyres flashed through her mind. 'Which way did he go?'

George pointed vaguely in the direction of Nesfield town before he turned away to take money from his next customer. 'He went thataway.'

'Did you see where exactly?' Helen asked.

The customer handed over a plastic card, then signed a piece of paper.

'Tut-tut. Don't you think I've got better things to do with my time than look out for one of your pesky cats?' George grumbled.

This was all the twins were likely to get out of him, they realised. So they decided the best plan was to race on.

'This way!' Hannah cried, sprinting past the giant petrol signs and straight through the open door of a small souvenir shop which was set back from the main road.

'Hey-up!' the lady behind the counter said as first Hannah, then Helen burst in. She was small and plump, with short fair hair and a smiley mouth. 'Am I seeing double, or what?'

'No, we're twins!' Helen gasped. 'We're looking for a white kitten. Did you see him?'

'Now let me see.' The woman took her time, sorting through a pile of colourful postcards as she pondered. 'We don't get that many kittens buying souvenirs!'

'Did you notice one running past the door about ten minutes ago?' Hannah stuck to the point. 'If so, which way was he heading?'

'I'm sorry, I'm teasing you.' The shop lady came out from behind her counter and took them to the door. 'I did catch a glimpse of your kitten, and I remember thinking he was too little to be out and about on a main road.'

'Oh!' Helen put a hand over her eyes and groaned. This situation was getting worse by the second. 'Don't say Mitch got run over!'

The woman shook her head. 'No. Luckily, he didn't stick to the road. He took off round the side of my shop, up the hill at the back.' She took them outside to show them. 'You see that footpath running alongside the stone wall? I can see it through the side window of my shop, and as a matter of fact, I spotted your kitten strolling along the top of the wall as if he didn't have a care in the world.'

Hannah nodded. 'Where does the path lead to?'

'It comes out at Peter and Alice Elton's place, The Evergreens.'

'Of course!' Helen heaved a sigh of relief that Mitch had chosen to run to the boarding kennels. It was a safer route for his adventure than the busy main road. She thanked the souvenir shop lady and dragged Hannah off up the path.

'Thank goodness we're on the right track,' Hannah muttered. She felt that the kennel owners might even have spotted the runaway, recognised him and tempted him into the house. At this very minute, it was possible that Alice or Peter was phoning Lucy at Stonelea with the good news that Mitch had been found.

'On the right track *so far*!' Helen glanced over the wall at acres of sloping green fields which led up to rocky Rydal Fell and miles of wild countryside. 'But what if Mitch took it into his head to go and explore the mountains?'

'Don't even think about it!' Hannah gritted her teeth and ran on until the Eltons' modern bungalow came into view. 'What time is it?' she gasped.

'Time you got a watch.'

'Ha-ha. Seriously, how long have we got before Joanna Day comes to pick Mitch up?'

'Three hours,' Helen reported. 'Look, here's Alice walking some of the dogs!'

A middle-aged woman in green wellies and a dark waxed jacket appeared at the top of the narrow path surrounded by a posse of small King Charles spaniels. The five dogs were all on leads, yapping and criss-crossing so that they tangled themselves in knots and Alice had to stoop to free them.

'Girls, am I pleased to see you!' she said when she straightened up and saw the twins running to meet her. 'I don't suppose you fancy a spot of dog-walking by the lake?'

The five spaniels yapped and tangled themselves up again, their long black-and-tan coats gleaming. *Yap-yap, yap-yap, wrughh!*

'We'd love to but we can't!' Hannah gabbled. 'We've lost a black-and-white kitten. He headed this way. Did you see him?'

'Uh-oh; emergency!' Knowing the situation at Stonelea, with Lucy laid up by her accident, Alice quickly realised what was going on. 'No, I haven't seen an escaped cat, but Peter's working in the kennels. Why not run and ask him?'

Helen nodded. 'Sorry we can't help with the dogs!'

'Next time!' Hannah promised.

So they ran on. The yaps grew fainter as Alice and her mob of spaniels disappeared round a bend. Ahead, standing on a hill overlooking a small lake, was The Evergreens.

The bungalow was neat and clean. There was a trimmed laurel hedge down the side of the drive, and out of sight round the back of the house was a long, low wooden building where the Eltons boarded their doggy guests.

'Quick!' Helen felt they were losing time. Mitch had had at least a fifteen minutes start on them, and by this time he could be anywhere. 'Pray that Mr Elton saw him!' she whispered to Hannah as they skirted round the back of the bungalow. If not, the trail would have gone well and truly cold.

Yap-yap! Yap-yap! Yap-yap-yap! A new chorus of excited dogs began at the sound of two pairs of hurried footsteps approaching across the gravel yard.

'Be quiet, Roly! Get down, Henrietta! You lot have already made quite enough fuss for one morning!' Peter Elton's voice rose above the din. Then he appeared in the kennel doorway.

'Mr Elton . . .' Hannah's lungs ached from running up the long hill. She sucked in air and bent double.

'. . . Have you . . .' Helen gasped.

'. . . Seen a . . .'

'. . . Black-and-white kitten?'

Between them they managed to get out the vital question.

Peter closed the door behind him to shut out

the din. A chubby man with a bald head, round cheeks and a white beard, he quickly put the twins out of their misery. 'I did see a kitten,' he told them. 'About ten minutes ago. Roly and the others kicked up a dreadful fuss so I came outside into the yard to see what it was all about. Nearly tripped over the little monkey . . . what's his name?'

'Mitch!' they both replied. Their brown eyes were large and shiny, their faces red, their dark hair sticking to their foreheads. 'He went missing from Stonelea!'

The Father Christmas look-alike nodded. 'I guessed as much. So I tried to corner the little blighter and shoo him inside the back door of the house before I called for reinforcements.'

Helen made a funny, frowning face at Hannah. Why couldn't adults say what they meant in plain English? 'What's a blighter?' she whispered out of the corner of her mouth.

'Never mind that now!' Hannah acted as if she knew the answers. She didn't. 'Does that mean you've got Mitch safe and sound?'

'Afraid not,' Mr Elton looked sorry to disappoint them. 'He's a slippery customer. I thought I had him trapped behind the tub of busy Lizzies, but when I made my move, he scampered up on to the top of the tub, trampled right through the flowers, then took a flying leap over my shoulder.'

'That sounds like typical Mitch,' Helen sighed.

Hannah groaned. 'Which way did he go?'

'Back down the footpath towards the main road,' the kennel owner told them with a glum face. 'I'm sorry to tell you, girls, that you've probably just wasted ten minutes of valuable time!'

'Don't give up!' Hannah urged. She knew that by this time they were at least half an hour behind runaway Mitch and that the minutes were slipping by without any new sign. But she was determined as ever to get him back before Joanna Day arrived at Stonelea. 'A kitten can't just vanish!'

'Mitch can!' To Helen, the world suddenly seemed a very large place in which to find one very small cat. She wished they had a giant loudspeaker to call out their message: *Help! Has anyone seen our cat?*

'No; the chase is still on!' Hannah insisted. Back on the main road, she slowed to a trot and peered over walls and under hedges, into the gardens of terraced houses, and up trees that overhung the pavement.

'My legs hurt,' Helen complained. They were thirty minutes behind Mitch and failing to close the gap. 'I don't think I can go much further.'

'Yeah, so we give in,' Hannah muttered scornfully. She'd spied a cat sitting on the roof of an outhouse, but it was big and ginger; definitely not Mitch. 'We go back to Stonelea and tell Joanna Day, "Sorry but we mislaid your kitten. Why not just choose another from the wide selection of attractive, homeless animals we have here?" '

'OK, OK!' Helen gritted her teeth and looked round for another person to ask.

'Have you . . .'

'. . . Seen a . . .'

'. . . Black-and-white kitten?'

'No, sorry.'

They ran on.

'Have you . . .? Have you . . .? Have you . . .?'

'No, sorry . . . Sorry . . . Sorry!'

'He *can't* have vanished into thin air!' Hannah repeated as they approached a small row of shops on the outskirts of town. There was a florist's with buckets of bright blooms standing outside the door. Then came a newsagent's with a stand of newspapers on display. The papers fluttered in the breeze as Helen and Hannah peered into the dark shop.

'Have you . . .'

'. . . Seen a . . .'

'Hannah, wait!' Helen grabbed her sister's arm and pointed wildly across the street.

Hannah saw a row of parked cars glinting in the sun and a terrace of similar shops. There was an off-licence, and next to it the chemist's, and next to that was the Fish Dish.

'Look!' Helen croaked.

'What am I looking at?' Hannah made out a small queue of people starting inside the fish-and-chip shop and trailing out under a buttercup-yellow awning which overhung the narrow pavement.

'The canopy!' Helen squeaked. She pointed frantically at a small, black-and-white furry shape asleep in the sun, then tugged at Hannah's arm to cross the street with her.

'Oh . . . my . . . gosh!' Hannah breathed. The

smell of fried fish entered her nostrils as they approached the shop.

'Late lunch!' Helen muttered darkly. 'We might have guessed.'

'Shh!' Hannah warned, as the queue for fish and chips shuffled forwards, unaware of who was sitting on the awning above their heads. 'Don't make him jump!'

'OK. We've gotta creep up on him without him seeing!' Helen agreed. She tiptoed stealthily between the parked cars and approached the Fish Dish at an angle.

'He's still snoozing!' Hannah murmured, squeezing between two people in the queue.

'Who is?' one boy said, craning his neck to see.

Helen stared at him as if it was the most obvious question in the world. 'Mitch!' she hissed back.

'Who's Mitch?' The boy stepped out of line to look up at the canopy.

'Our kitten!' With a finger to her lips, Hannah squinted into the dazzling sun.

Yes; it was Mitch all right. Cosy as you like on the warm yellow canvas. Black-and-white and fluffy, the end of his short tail twitching gently. Basking in the smell from the shop, probably dreaming of fish.

The kitten stirred and opened his eyes. He stood up and stretched. Then he padded down the slope, peered over the rim of the canopy . . . and spied Hannah and Helen, breaths held, staring anxiously back up at him.

Seven

'Grab that cat!' the nosy boy cried. He jumped up, caught hold of the edge of the canopy and swung there like a chimpanzee.

'Don't do that! You'll scare him!' Helen shrieked.

Too late. The canopy rocked, rattled and lurched like the Titanic hitting the iceberg.

'*Meee-owww!*' Mitch made a motorbike screech then launched himself into space.

Hannah almost blacked out in sheer surprise. Her head spun as she stared up into the blue sky and tried to follow the kitten's curved descent. Mitch's back was arched, his feet splayed. He landed safely on the soft top of a parked red convertible. '*Mi-aow!*'

'Quick, catch him before he . . .!' Helen's voice penetrated the whirl of confusion which Hannah found herself in.

Too late again. Mitch flicked his ears, then took off from the car roof. He leaped down to the pavement, scooted under the nosy boy's dangling legs, and through the startled queue of customers.

'He's heading into the chip shop!' someone cried.

'Stop him!'

'Grab him!'

'Trap him!'

'Don't let him escape!'

Mitch wove through the forest of legs. *Fish!* He was wide awake now, and he could still smell his favourite smell. *Fried haddock, battered plaice, breadcrumbed fillet of cod*. Tempted, licking his lips and drawn in by the promise of cat heaven, he paused in the doorway.

Helen thrust her way through the crowd. She hovered over the runaway kitten, ready to rugby-tackle him into submission. But a pair of dangling feet thudded into the small of her back as the boy dropped down from the canopy.

'Ouch!' Helen sprawled flat onto the tiled shop floor. Her nose slid up against the dull steel counter, where she caught her own fuzzy reflection.

And slippery Mitch snuck away before Helen hit the deck. He turned his back on *fish-fish-fish* and melted into the crowd of onlookers, who oohed and aahed, and dived and tackled in vain.

'He's getting away!' Hannah cried. She chased him along the pavement, keeping him carefully in sight. But she realised that Mitch was increasing his lead as she jostled people out of the way. 'C'mon, Helen!' she called. 'I just saw Mitch dart through that fence into the allotments. See him? He's in that lettuce patch!'

After Helen had scraped herself off the floor, she charged after her twin. Her knees were bruised, her pride in tatters. 'If Mitch thinks we're playing cat-and-mouse through someone else's vegetable patch, he's got another think coming!' she groaned.

'Here, kitty, kitty!' Hannah called, one leg over the fence, struggling for balance.

'*Kitty!*' Helen echoed savagely. She vaulted the fence and landed in a pile of something soft.

'Yuck!' A foul smell hit Hannah full in the face.

'Uurrgh!' Helen jumped clear. 'I'll "Kitty, kitty" that cat when I get hold of it!'

'You just fell into a heap of horse dung!' In spite of everything, Hannah yelped with laughter.

'It's manure, if you must know!' Helen glowered and wiped the soles of her trainers in some long grass. 'And if you tell anyone . . .!'

'I will!' Hannah promised, quick as a flash.

'Yeah, well, Miss Clever. You're so busy laughing at me that you've lost precious kitty again!' Jerking her thumb towards the neat rows of frilly green lettuce, Helen proved her point.

There was no Mitch crouching low and stalking between the plants, only a track of dainty paw-prints through the freshly dug soil.

So Hannah and Helen were forced to study the clues and pick up the trail anew.

'Here's a paw-print!' Hannah went between two raised rows of potatoes on her hands and knees.

'That's too big for a kitten,' Helen observed. 'More like a dog.'

'OK, here's another one.' Pointing to a small heap of soil and scratched earth, Hannah identified sure signs of cat.

'Over here!' Helen had scouted on ahead, through a patch of juicy strawberries. More pawprints led between rows of raspberry canes, into the cool shade of some rhubarb leaves.

'Mitch!' Hannah crouched by the broad, umbrella-shaped leaves and whispered softly. 'If you're good and come out nice and quietly, I promise you can have some lovely cod for supper!'

'That's bribery!' Helen hissed. She too crouched low and searched under the leaves, between the straight, thick, red stalks.

'Yep,' Hannah admitted. 'Lovely cod and pieces of salmon, and scrummy, yummy sardines!'

'*Mew-mew!*' A faint cry emerged from the rhubarb.

'That's right!' Helen got off her high horse and joined in the sly promises. 'Think supper, Mitch. Think kippers!'

'Kippers, my foot!' a loud voice barked.

Hannah and Helen looked up in alarm.

A tall man towered over them, sleeves rolled

up, wearing a broad leather belt buckled tight round his waist. 'What do you two think you're playing at?'

'We . . . we . . .' Helen stammered in surprise.

'We're looking for our cat,' Hannah whispered. Her words ran together in a muddle. 'Well, not ours exactly. And not a cat exactly either. More of a kitten . . .'

'On *my* allotment?' the gardener quizzed. He stood hands on hips, feet wide apart, boots caked with soil.

'We didn't mean . . .' Giving up all attempts at explanation, Helen abandoned her sentence and got slowly to her feet.

'Mitch is hiding in your rhubarb,' Hannah said lamely.

'In *my* rhubarb?' the man echoed.

('He had a face a bit like a parrot,' Helen recalled later when she told her mum the details. 'Y'know; with that beaky nose and beady eyes. Maybe that's why he repeated everything Hannah said.'

'Don't be rude.' Mary hid a smile in order to tell her off.

'Well, he did,' Hannah insisted. 'His chin tilted

up and his nose pointed down. Just like a parrot.')

'We're trying to persuade the kitten to come out,' Hannah said now, standing up and wiping earth from her hands.

'Persuade him?' Parrot-Face chirped, in his squeaky voice. 'I'll *persuade* him with the flat of my spade if you like!'

So saying, he lifted a long-handled garden spade out of the soil and swung it back like an axe, ready to strike.

'Oh no!' Hannah cried. 'Mitch, look out!'

'Don't hit him!' Helen pleaded. 'Think of your rhubarb!'

'My rhubarb!' the man said with a frown. He lowered the spade and thought again. 'You're right. Patch! Come here, boy!'

A small white, short-haired, sharp-nosed terrier shot out of the nearby garden shed like a bolt from the blue. His feet hardly touched the ground as he galloped between the potato drills, tail up, pink tongue lolling.

'Cat!' his master squawked and pointed at the rhubarb. 'Fetch!'

Unable to watch any longer, Hannah closed her

eyes. Instead of nibbling his way through a saucer of salmon for supper, it looked like Mitch was about to become a hungry dog's dinner.

Patch listened to the command, then darted into the green-and-red jungle with unerring aim.

'That's the job. Flush him out, Patch!' the proud gardener cried. 'Make him run for his life.'

'But Mitch is only little!' Helen cried in a broken voice. 'He's not doing any harm.'

'Not doing any harm!' The gardener sounded as though he was being strangled. His face was flushed crimson, his beady eyes bulging. 'Go on, Patch, I've had enough trouble with cats lately! You teach him never to trespass in my allotment ever again!'

'So the dog attacked Mitch!' Helen told her mum at the Curlew Café.

It was four o'clock. Two hours to go, and the countdown to six was continuing relentlessly. Helen and Hannah had scrambled out of the allotment after a fleeing Mitch, desperate not to allow him out of their sight.

The terrified cat had raced out of the rhubarb

with Patch close on his heels. He'd bounded up the nearest tree; a tall ash growing on the boundary between the allotment and Riverside Park.

Patch had barked himself hoarse, hurled himself at the tree, run himself dizzy round and round the wide trunk.

'Mitch was terrified!' Hannah explained. 'His fur stood on end and he was trembling all over.'

Both girls slumped exhausted into chairs at a café table.

Mary listened carefully and pieced together the story as best she could. 'And where is Mitch now?' she asked.

'Still up the tree,' Helen told her. She sagged forward, elbows on the table, her head in her hands. 'Or *was* when we last saw him.'

'So shouldn't you be there, keeping watch?'

Hannah nodded. 'Except Parrot-Face set his dog on us too,' she explained. 'Even after we climbed out of his smelly old allotment, he still sent Patch after us. And you know what terriers can be like. He snapped and snarled at our heels until we were forced to move away from the ash tree.'

'So we decided to come here until the man calls off his dog.' Still drooping, Helen groaned and sighed. 'Then we can go back and start all over again. But we've only got two hours left, Mum. We need some help.'

Mary agreed. 'But the bit I still don't understand is the part about Mitch and the tree. Why are you so sure he'll still be there when you go back?'

'Because . . .' Hannah began.

'Because it's a very big tree,' Helen explained. 'And Mitch is a very small cat.'

Mary gasped and a look of realisation flickered in to her sympathetic eyes. 'In other words . . .?'

'Yeah!' Helen sighed.

Hannah let her head drop right forward against the table and moaned out loud. 'Mitch is *stuck* up the tree!' she confirmed. 'And when I say stuck, I mean he really, really, really can't get down!'

Eight

'Cold drinks all round!' Mary Moore announced Step One in her plan to rescue Mitch. She produced lemonade which fizzed and sparkled in the glass.

Helen gulped it down. 'Phew, that's better!'

Step Two was to phone David at Home Farm.

'Hi, Dad.' Hannah launched into an explanation of the problem. 'We need a ladder to climb an ash tree. A long ladder. The longest one you can possibly bring.'

'Hmm. Are you absolutely sure that the kitten is stuck up the tree?' David ummed and aahed.

'Dad, it's a massive tree! Mitch only managed to

95

climb it because he was scared to death of the dog that was chasing him!' She recalled the smooth, straight trunk which eventually branched out into a wide canopy of thick leaves. The kitten had dug in his claws and scrambled up, then vanished along a high branch. The twins had gazed up from below, waiting anxiously for him to reappear. Meanwhile, the gardener's dog had chased them noisily out of the allotment in a flurry of snaps and growls.

Hannah's dad considered the situation. 'OK, listen. I'll put my longest ladder on the roof-rack of the car and drive over to Nesfield. Where did you say this tree was?'

'Between the allotments and Riverside Park. It's giant. You can't miss it.' She nodded in Helen's direction to let her know that the plan was moving ahead.

'Gotcha.' Sounding ready to leap into action, David told Hannah that he would see them in about an hour.

'Sooner if you can,' she pleaded, glancing at the clock behind the counter. It was almost four o'clock. 'We need to get Mitch back home by six!'

'In your dreams!'

'No, *really* Dad . . .!' The deadline was approaching far too quickly.

'I'll do my best,' David promised, putting down the phone to go and carry out his part of the plan.

'OK, what would be best to try and tempt a cat down from a tree?' Mary said next, rooting about in her glass-fronted refrigerator. 'A dish of double cream?'

'Fish!' Helen and Hannah said, quick as a flash.

'Fish? . . . How about fresh salmon?' Their mum produced a juicy pink portion from the fridge.

'Perfect!' Helen grabbed the small plastic container and covered it in cling-film.

'I still think the tree is too tall for Mitch to climb down,' Hannah pointed out. She was a couple of steps behind Helen, who, revived by the lemonade, was already halfway out of the café door. 'But thanks anyway, Mum.'

Mary smiled anxiously. 'Yes, and you be careful,' she warned. 'I don't want either of you to risk life and limb over Mitch. So, if the fish doesn't do the trick, you must wait for your father to arrive.'

'Then *he* can risk life and limb!' Hannah suggested wih a quick grin.

'Exactly!' Her mum shooed her out of the door. She waved them both off as they sprinted across the cobbled town square towards the park. 'Good luck!' she called.

'Thanks!' Gratefully clutching Mitch's salmon treat, Helen hurried on ahead of Hannah.

The tinkle of the café door as it closed told them they were on their own again. On their own until their dad arrived with the ladder. Two hours to go, and counting!

'Here, Mitch! Here, kitty!' Helen craned her neck and gazed up at the intricate pattern made by the branches.

Nothing moved, except a breeze through the feathery leaves.

'Lovely fish!' Hannah called, watching Helen waft the container through the air. 'Your favourite!'

Silence.

'Perhaps he managed to get down while we were at the café!' Helen whispered. She tried gazing up and offering the treat from a fresh angle on the allotment side of the fence.

'No way!' Hannah was convinced that the kitten was still cowering on a branch. 'He's hiding. We just have to be patient, that's all.'

'At least Parrot-Face and Patch have gone away,' Helen murmured, glancing across the empty squares of allotment.

'Wait, I think I saw Mitch!' Hannah cried. She pointed towards the end of a slim branch that seemed to be weighed down by the kitten's presence. Looking harder, she made out a small white face with big green eyes. 'Yes!'

'Where? Where?' Helen had to climb back over the fence to get a view of the runaway. When she saw him peering down from the swaying branch, she gasped. 'How high is that?'

'Don't ask!' *Very high. Very dangerous*. Hannah shuddered. 'Maybe one of us could try climbing up without waiting for the ladder?' she suggested faintly through gritted teeth.

'I thought you said Mum said we shouldn't?' Helen butted in.

'So?' Hannah turned on her for a moment. 'Are you chicken?'

Helen nodded.

'Me too!' Letting go of the tough act, Hannah sighed and stared up again at the kitten's precarious position. 'Did you hear that?'

'*Miaow-miaow!*'

'Yep.' Helen caught the frightened little sound coming from on high. It drifted down on the breeze and made her feel almost sick with worry for Mitch. So she raised the salmon treat again, and held it up so that he could see. 'Nice fish!' she coaxed. 'Yum-yum!'

'Come on, Mitch; you can do it!' Hannah urged.

'*Miaow!*' The kitten crouched on the thin branch, clinging on as it bent and swayed.

'No he can't!' she murmured in despair.

She grabbed Helen's wrist to look at her watch. Four-thirty. Where had their dad got to? Why wasn't he here?

'What's the problem?' A man wheeling a barrow emerged from a greenhouse and caught sight of the girls as he made his way down a narrow path. 'Cat stuck up the tree, is it?'

'Oh no, not another Parrot-Face!' Helen whispered. She and Hannah stood shoulder to

shoulder on the far side of the fence, expecting to be shooed off for a second time.

'Looks more like a lion!' Hannah mumbled, on the lookout for another unfriendly dog.

The man was young and sturdy, with a big mane of wavy fair hair and a beard to match. His fawn T-shirt, beige trousers and sandy coloured desert boots had added to Hannah's impression that the newcomer was the king of the jungle.

'It's OK, I won't bite,' the man promised. He put down the barrow and trod carefully between the rows of vegetables. 'I thought I heard a cat up the tree a bit earlier, but I couldn't see exactly what the problem was.'

'He went up there about an hour ago,' Helen explained shyly. 'A terrier chased him off the allotments.'

'Ah, that would be Tom Leyburn's dog. Tom doesn't like cats mucking about amongst his lettuces.' The stranger looked up and spotted Mitch's refuge. 'Oh my, I see what you mean!'

'Do you think he'll fall?' Helen asked.

The man shook his head. 'Not unless the wind gets up a bit. Cats have great balance, remember. By the way, my name's Will.'

So Patch belongs to a man called Leyburn! Hannah frowned deeply as she pondered. *Leyburn? Where do I remember that name from?*

'Hann, Will says we could try shinning up the trunk and shaking the branch!' Helen broke into Hannah's train of thought. 'Doing that might make Mitch go back towards the centre of the tree and we might be able to reach him!'

'Who's doing the climbing?' Hannah reminded her.

'Hmm. Good point.'

Will stared up at the smooth, straight trunk. 'Yeah, forget that idea. Too difficult. But I do have a back-up plan. There's this theory that a wet cat will always come down to the ground.'

'But it's not raining,' Hannah pointed out. In fact, the sky was bright blue, with only a few wispy clouds on the rugged horizon.

'*Miaow! Miaow! Miaow!*' Mitch's cries grew louder and more fed-up. *Get me down, please!*

'I'm not talking about rain.' The helpful newcomer with the deep, growly voice and shock of hair explained his plan. 'You see the green garden hose running from that water tap? I could run it over here and point the nozzle up into the ash tree. I reckon the jet will just about reach the branch where the kitten is. What do you think?'

'You mean, you want to squirt water at Mitch?' Helen tried to get this straight in her mind.

'Mmm. That's the general idea.'

'But why?' Hannah too had trouble getting her head around this. 'Won't it just scare him and make him cold and wet?'

'No, because like I said, it's a proven theory. It's even something I saw the fire service do one time.

The jet from their hose brought down a cat that had been stuck up a tree for five whole days.'

Helen nodded. 'Worth a try?' she asked Hannah.

'I guess.' *A wet cat comes down*, she repeated, to remind herself why they were doing this.

So Will went to trail the hose across to the base of the tree, handing the nozzle to Helen, then retracing his steps to the tap by Tom Leyburn's garden shed. 'Ready?' he called.

'*Mee-oww! Mee-oww!*' Mitch cried in growing alarm. From his bird's-eye view, all the kitten could see was a long, bright-green hose snaking across the allotment below.

Helen took a deep breath. 'Ready!'

'A wet cat comes down,' Hannah repeated out loud. She crossed her fingers and half-closed her eyes. If only adventurous Mitch hadn't got himself into this mess to begin with!

'Here goes!' Will turned on the tap full-blast.

Rrrr-rrr-whoosh! Water spouted out of the nozzle and rose in a high arc. The jet hit the leaves, broke up and splattered back down on Helen and Hannah's heads.

'*Miaowwww!*' Mitch heard the water shooting

up from below. He quickly turned on his narrow branch and scrambled back towards the trunk.

'It's working!' Helen cried amidst the soaking she was getting. 'Yes, yes . . . yes . . . No!'

The kitten reached the main trunk and dug in his claws. He shot further up the tree to a higher branch still.

'A . . . wet . . . cat . . . comes . . . down,' Hannah grumbled. Her hair was dripping, her T-shirt was soaked through. 'Yeah! Like . . . yeah!'

'Hmm.' Will came over to study the disappointing results of his wet-cat-comes-down theory.

'Mitch climbed further up to get out of the range of the water!' Helen said in disgust, dropping the hose. The strong jet made the hose squirm around, then snake towards Will's legs.

'So he did,' the gardener admitted. He jumped a mile as the cold jet blasted his ankles.

'But here comes Dad!' Hannah cried. She heard the car and spotted the long ladder on its roof.

'At last!' Helen left Will to cope with the crazy hose and ran to greet David. 'Dad, it's getting worse. Mitch went even higher up the tree! *And* we're all soaked!'

'Whoa!' David steadied both girls as he unstrapped the ladder. 'I can see you're wet. But tell me about it later. For now, just lend a hand.'

Together they took the weight of the ladder and heaved it from the rack. Then they balanced it, and the three of them carried it across the corner of the park towards the ash tree.

'Here!' Hannah gasped. The ladder was heavy and unwieldy, difficult to prop upright against the trunk.

'Steady!' David called, nodding a brief hello at Will. 'Move it left a bit so we're on level ground. Now let it go gently against the tree. Don't let it land with a thud. That's right!'

'Is that as high as it goes?' Hannah looked up in disappointment to see that the top of the ladder didn't even reach the place where the strong trunk began to branch off.

'Afraid so.' David too stood back. He judged the distance between the ladder and the high spot Mitch had chosen. 'Not so good, huh?'

Helen's hopes plummeted. And now, to make things worse, she spotted the familiar figure of Parrot-Face, minus his dog, stamping across the allotment towards them. She nudged Hannah with her elbow and bit her lip.

'But it's worth a try,' their gallant dad decided, setting foot on the bottom rung of the ladder and asking Will to stand there to hold it steady. He climbed quickly to the top, then stretched to see if he could grab hold of the sturdy lowest branch. 'Nearly!' he cried, reaching with his fingertips.

'What's going on here?' Tom Leyburn demanded. He laid a hand on Will's shoulder and tried to wrench him away.

'Watch out, Dad!' Helen cried as the ladder shook and wobbled.

'I've got it!' Stretching to his limit, David managed to catch hold of the branch. But he was off-balance when the ladder began to shake. His foot slipped from the top rung.

'Dad!' Hannah screamed.

The ladder slipped sideways. David hung in midair.

In the topmost branches of the ash tree Mitch cried out in panic and clung on for dear life.

Nine

'Wow, look at that!' Hannah gazed up into the tree open-mouthed.

David had swung from the branch, and for two seconds it looked as if he might lose his grip and fall. But he'd got over the fright and now he was swinging his legs up towards the branch and gripping it with his ankles. He hung suspended like a cuddly koala to catch his breath. Then he rocked his whole body sideways until he could roll himself round the branch and come out on top.

'Amazing!' Helen breathed. Since when had their dad been an Olympic-class gymnast?

Meanwhile, Lionheart Will fought off an angry Tom Leyburn.

'Hey, watch what you're doing!' the young gardener called. 'Can't you see there's a bloke at the top of this thing?'

The ladder had already toppled sideways and come to rest against the branch of a smaller, neighbouring tree. But now Will scuffled free of Tom to go and rescue it. He heaved and leaned it in its original position. 'OK!' he called up to David. 'The ladder's back in place. You can come down when you're ready!'

'Right you are!' The twins' dad sat on the branch to steady himself. 'Just give me a couple of minutes!'

'Thank goodness he's all right!' Hannah whispered. She scowled openly at the confused old man who'd almost managed to get their dad killed.

'What . . .? Why . . .? How . . .?' Tom stammered. The colour had drained from his beaky face. 'I'd no idea anyone was up there!'

'Maybe he should've checked first, before he began throwing his weight around,' Helen muttered.

'I just recognised these kids from earlier this afternoon.' Tom tried to excuse his reckless action. 'They'd been swarming over my rhubarb, looking for some cat or other. So I saw red, I admit.'

'The cat's up the tree,' Will explained in short, easy words.

'Up the tree?' Parrot-Face repeated. A look of realisation dawned in his beady eyes as he spotted David setting foot back on the ladder. Way up above, Mitch's white face could be seen peering down on all the excitement.

'Cat!' Tom said, putting two and two together at last. 'Oh dear . . . Oh no! Now look here, I'm very sorry!'

'Careful, Dad!' Helen called as David descended one rung at a time.

'I'm OK,' he told her, though his voice sounded shaky.

'It's been a bad week for cats,' shame-faced Tom mumbled. 'Show me a cat and I'll show you a problem.'

'Are you talking about your John's little lad's pet moggy?' Will asked, one eye still on David's descent.

'Yes, Tiger. Ever since John and his family came to stay, there's been nothing but trouble. My whole week has been ruined!'

'So you didn't find the missing mog?' Will murmured.

Mog . . .? Missing . . .? Tiger . . .? Hannah gave the conversation her full attention.

'Leyburn!' Helen squealed. She squeezed Hannah's arm so hard that Hannah squeaked too. 'We worked out that Mrs Leyburn is Mark's grandma, remember! That means Mr Leyburn is Mrs Leyburn's husband and Mark's grandad! John is Mr and Mrs Leyburn's son, and Mark's dad!'

'And Corporal isn't Corporal; he's Tiger!' Hannah exclaimed.

Wow, were they both brilliant, or what? Their eyes gleamed and they jumped up and down.

Will and the old man turned from the ladder to stare.

'When did Corp— Tiger go missing?' Hannah needed to check to be quite sure.

'Let's see. It must be three days since. Mark and the three other kiddies cried for hours on end about it. John and I looked everywhere, but there was no sign of him. We reckon it was because the cat didn't know the territory. He must've wandered off and got lost. Mark's mummy promised to buy him another kitten, but even that didn't help.' Tom Leyburn gave them the information they were longing to hear.

'Is Tiger a tabby cat?' Helen asked, just to be doubly certain.

'. . . Hey, what about your poor old dad?' David complained as he reached the bottom rung of the ladder and Will stepped to one side. 'Don't I deserve a hero's welcome when I make it back to Planet Earth?'

'Hang on, Dad!' Hannah twitched and fretted for Tom's final answer.

'Tabbies are the stripy ones?' Mark's grandad checked.

Helen and Hannah nodded and held their breaths.

'That's Tiger,' Tom confirmed. 'And in my opinion, he was more trouble than he was worth!'

* * *

'That's one mystery solved,' David said when he could finally make sense of the girls' breathless explanations.

Mr Leyburn had finished apologising, then hurried off to pass on the good news to his grandchildren. Kind-hearted Will was busy tidying up the allotments after the excitement. It was half-past five and they were no nearer to rescuing the kitten.

'You were great up that tree, Dad!' Hannah put her arm round his waist and squeezed. 'I'd give you a score of nine point five!'

'Out of ten?' He squeezed her shoulder. 'Would I have got full marks if I'd brought Mitch down with me?'

'Yes, but it's not your fault.' She gazed up to the top branches, searching for the kitten amongst the fluttering leaves.

'*Miaow!*' came the short, sharp, hungry cry.

'There!' Helen saw and pointed. She picked up the forgotten fish treat and waved it in Mitch's direction.

The green eyes in the small white face focused intently on the salmon. Mitch shifted his position

Mitch Goes Missing

and came into full view. The branch swayed and bent under his weight.

'Watch out!' Hannah ran to the base of the trunk and called up in alarm.

The kitten hadn't flinched. His eyes were still on the fish.

'Here, Mitch! Here, kitty!' Helen chanted.

The adventurer moved again. He backed off slowly towards a larger branch, took a swift look behind him and worked himself down to a lower level and a stouter limb.

'Ohhhh!' Hannah looked away.

'*Miaooww!*' Mitch slid smoothly from one branch to the next, lower and lower, more and more rapidly as the smell of the salmon filled his nostrils.

'Look at that!' a stunned David said.

'Shh!' Helen warned. 'That's right, Mitch! The game's over. Time to come down. Easy does it!'

Lithe as a panther, sleek as a leopard, the kitten climbed down the tree. His eyes flashed out of the shade, his purr grew louder as he prepared to leap the last three metres.

'B-b-but . . .' Hannah protested. '. . . I thought you couldn't get down!'

From his vertical position, Mitch leaned back on his haunches and prepared to jump.

'Lovely fish!' Helen sang out. 'Here, kitty, kitty! Here, Mitch!'

'And he jumped down and he noshed the food all in one go!' Helen told Lucy Carlton.

'So he wasn't stuck after all?' The old lady's face wrinkled into a broad smile as she watched Hannah run a comb through the kitten's fur to make him spick and span.

'No. He had us fooled, though,' Helen admitted.

'And David, you were the hero?' Lucy welcomed Corporal on to her lap by the kitchen door. She stroked him and made a big fuss.

'Almost the hero who was joining you on a pair of crutches!' he grinned sheepishly.

'What time is it?' Hannah murmured, combing and smoothing Mitch until his soft fur was fluffy and white.

'*Mew-mew!*' he complained, flicking his tail and crouching bad-temperedly on Hannah's knee.

'Time-you-got-a-watch-five-to-six!' Helen gabbled.

'Phew, five minutes to go. Who's that coming down the path now?' Hannah heard the click of the gate and footsteps approaching. 'Is it Joanna Day?'

'No, it's the Leyburns,' a man's voice called from the kitchen doorway. 'I'm John, and this is Mark. We've come to collect Tiger!'

Hearing John speak, the tabby cat pricked up his ears. He jumped down from the Cat Lady's lap and padded quickly across the stone floor.

Mark appeared in front of his father. 'Tiger!'

'*Meee-ow!*' The cat called out a soft, high greeting. He walked right up to the red-headed boy and wound himself between his legs.

'I knew it was you on the poster!' Mark whispered. 'So I just wished and wished you'd come back – and you did!'

'Thanks to Hannah and Helen,' Lucy reminded John Leyburn.

'Not really!' Overcome by modesty, Helen rushed to the gate to look out for Joanna Day.

Hannah picked Mitch up and followed her. The

kitten squirmed and wriggled in her arms. 'Oh no you don't!' she told him. 'You're not going anywhere!'

'Here she comes!' Helen spotted a silver car pulling into the small carpark by the stream.

A tanned young woman with brown, bobbed hair, wearing jeans and a strappy top, got out and ran towards them. 'Mitch!' she cried.

The black-and-white kitten gave a miaow of pleasure.

'Here I am! Did you think I'd left you for ever?' Joanna took him from Hannah. 'Oh, poor little thing. Did you miss me?'

Helen coughed. 'I'm sure he did!'

The woman smiled and cuddled her kitten. 'And have you behaved yourself? Have you been good?'

It was Hannah's turn to swallow. 'As good as gold,' she told Mitch's owner.

Not a word about Mitch going missing.

The kitten turned his angelic white face towards the twins and flashed them a look with his beautiful green eyes.

Both Hannah and Helen could've sworn that his

119

whiskers twitched and his pink mouth curled up at the corners in a broad, contented, *thanks-a-million* smile.

STAR THE SURPRISE
Home Farm Twins 20

Jenny Oldfield

Meet Helen and Hannah. They're identical twins – and mad about the animals on their Lake District farm!

A thoroughbred foal is born at a livery stables near Doveton – surprising everyone with her early arrival! Hannah and Helen only just get there in time to watch. Now she needs special care, and the twins are willing volunteers. Left in charge while her owner is away, Star springs another surprise on them by disappearing. Has she run away, or is it theft? The twins only have twenty four hours to find out!

HORSES OF HALF-MOON RANCH
Midnight Lady

Jenny Oldfield

Watching a neighbouring rancher break in new horses, Kirstie is horrified by the treatment of one strong-willed mare, Midnight Lady. In a desperate bid to free her, Kirstie pays a secret night-time visit to the ranch. But the plan back-fires: not one, but eight horses escape and disappear into the mountains! Now Kirstie is in big trouble – should she own up? And if she does, will she ever see Midnight Lady again?

HOME FARM TWINS
Jenny Oldfield

66127 5	Speckle The Stray	£3.99	❏
66128 3	Sinbad The Runaway	£3.99	❏
66129 1	Solo The Homeless	£3.99	❏
66130 5	Susie The Orphan	£3.99	❏
66131 3	Spike The Tramp	£3.99	❏
66132 1	Snip and Snap The Truants	£3.99	❏
68990 0	Sunny The Hero	£3.99	❏
68991 9	Socks The Survivor	£3.99	❏
68992 7	Stevie The Rebel	£3.99	❏
68993 5	Samson The Giant	£3.99	❏
69983 3	Sultan The Patient	£3.99	❏
69984 1	Sorrel The Substitute	£3.99	❏
69985 X	Skye The Champion	£3.99	❏
69986 8	Sugar and Spice The Pickpockets	£3.99	❏
69987 6	Sophie The Show-off	£3.99	❏
72682 2	Smoky The Mystery	£3.99	❏
72795 0	Scott The Braveheart	£3.99	❏
72796 9	Spot The Prisoner	£3.99	❏
727977	Shelley The Shadow	£3.99	❏

All Hodder Children's books are available at your local bookshop, or can be ordered direct from the publisher. Just tick the titles you would like and complete the details below. Prices and availability are subject to change without prior notice.

Please enclose a cheque or postal order made payable to *Bookpoint Ltd*, and send to: Hodder Children's Books, 39 Milton Park, Abingdon, OXON OX14 4TD, UK. Email Address: orders@bookpoint.co.uk

If you would prefer to pay by credit card, our call centre team would be delighted to take your order by telephone. Our direct line *01235 400414* (lines open 9.00 am–6.00 pm Monday to Saturday, 24 hour message answering service). Alternatively you can send a fax on *01235 400454*.

TITLE		FIRST NAME		SURNAME	

ADDRESS	
DAYTIME TEL:		POST CODE	

If you would prefer to pay by credit card, please complete:
Please debit my Visa/Access/Diner's Card/American Express (delete as applicable) card no:

Signature .... Expiry Date: ....

If you would NOT like to receive further information on our products please tick the box. ❏